THE
YEAR
OF
MR.
NOBODY

by Cynthia King

Illustrated by Malcolm Carrick

Harper & Row, Publishers
New York, Hagerstown, San Francisco, London

For Mellie

THE YEAR OF MR. NOBODY
Text copyright © 1978 by Cynthia King
Illustrations copyright © 1978 by Malcolm Carrick

FIRST EDITION

Library of Congress Cataloging in Publication Data
King, Cynthia.
  The year of Mr. Nobody.

  SUMMARY: A little boy gradually outgrows his
dependence on his imaginary friend.
  I. Carrick, Malcolm.   II. Title.
PZ7.K5758Ye   [E]   77–11830
ISBN 0–06–023132–7
ISBN 0–06–023133–5 lib. bdg.

Contents

1 August • Measuring Up

The year began at summer's end, just two days after Abbot's birthday. This was his first trip to the Amusement Park. He loved the noise, the tinny music, the Popsicles, the rides.

He loved the little car he could pedal and steer. He bumped smack into his big brother Evan's car, wham bang! Evan laughed and bumped him back.

He loved the airplane that went round and round, up and down. His stomach went round and round, up and down too. When he climbed out he couldn't walk straight.

"Now," said Evan, "for the Cyclone." Abbot had seen the high looping track of the roller coaster. He had heard the whanging sound of the train clackety-clacking over the trellises. He got in line behind Evan.

"I'll wait out here," Mother said. "Evan, hold tight to Abbot."

"Why aren't you going?" Abbot asked.

"I rode my last Cyclone twenty years ago," Mother said firmly.

1

"Mother's scared," Evan explained. Abbot thought it strange that a grown-up who wasn't afraid to walk straight into giant breakers at the ocean was afraid of anything so much fun as a roller coaster.

"I'm not scared," he said.

Through the gate he could see children climbing into the cars of the train that waited at the platform. A guard was taking tickets and checking safety belts. Evan went through the gate and got in one of the cars. Abbot started through after him.

"Wait a minute." A man put his big arm in front of Abbot's chin. "You can't go in there."

"Why not? I have my ticket."

"You're too small."

"But I just had my birthday!"

The man pointed to a red stripe somewhere over Abbot's head on the side of the gate. "See, sonny, you've got to be up to the red line. That's the rule."

Abbot stretched his neck and stood on tiptoe.

The man shook his head. "Sonny, you just don't measure up."

Abbot couldn't think of anything to say. He stood next to Mother and put his chin on the railing. He saw a green Popsicle melting on the sidewalk, and dirty hot-dog wrappers in the grass. The sun was too hot, the tinny music too loud.

He felt Mother's hand on his shoulder. "I didn't know about the red line," she said. "I guess unless you're a certain height they're afraid you'll fall out."

"I wouldn't fall out," Abbot said.

"We'll come back next year when you're bigger."

"I'm bigger now. Father said so when he measured me." Abbot moved out from under her hand.

If I were invisible, he thought, *I could just have walked right through that gate and no one would know. I could be sitting next to Evan now.*

Evan's train started slowly up the first hill. Abbot opened his eyes wide watching it. At the top it hesitated, then plunged down the track and raced around so fast it was a blur. Seconds later it raced by him and stopped. Evan came out unsteadily. His eyes were like two glass marbles. *Evan wouldn't have been scared if I'd been there holding on to him,* Abbot thought.

It wasn't fair. No matter what he wanted to do he was either too young or too small. For the rest of the day, even when they were on the carousel and the Ferris wheel, all Abbot could think about was the roller coaster rushing around without him.

Father came home early that night, so they had dinner in the dining room with candles on the table. Mother dished up the vegetables, and Evan kept saying, "May I start?" They always passed first to Evan because he was the oldest.

Sandy, in his high chair, picked up a carrot with his fingers, though Mother made Abbot eat with a fork.

3

Father said, "Why so glum, Abbot?"

"He didn't measure up," Evan said before Abbot had a chance to answer. "May I start?"

"He didn't measure up," said Sandy, who always said what anybody else said.

Father raised his eyebrows. "Abbot, what's all this about?"

Abbot opened his mouth to tell Father about the red line and to ask him why forty-two inches wasn't tall enough, but his voice didn't work.

Mother said quickly, "You may start, Evan." Then she told Father about the rule. Evan talked about the rides. Sandy sang, "Measure up, measure up."

Abbot sat still, smelling the dinner he couldn't eat. He wished he could say something. He wished he were invisible so he could fly about the ceiling or anywhere else he wanted. He swallowed and watched the flickering candles.

One of the candles was shorter than the other. It would burn to nothing, he thought, while the other was still tall.

While Mother passed her plate to Father for some meat and told Evan not to talk with his mouth full, Abbot blew out the low candle.

"Why did the candle go out?" Evan asked.

"Why did the candle go out?" asked Sandy.

"Mr. Nobody blew it out," Abbot announced.

"Who?" they all said together. Everyone looked at him.

Abbot giggled. "Mr. Nobody blew it out," he explained, "because that candle was just too short. It didn't measure up."

Everyone in the family got used to Mr. Nobody except Mother. She said, "Frankly, I don't like Mr. Nobody. He's a troublemaker." Abbot knew Mr. Nobody didn't start trouble. He just came when trouble came.

"Also," Mother said, "he's a figment of your imagination, yet you talk about him as if he's real. I don't know who you think you are, Abbot Sanderson Dodge or Mr. Nobody."

Abbot didn't know either. He'd only just made him up. It takes time to know all about someone, even someone who isn't there.

Evan's first day back at school was a bad day for Abbot. He spent the morning on the front porch waiting for Evan, waiting for lunch, and wishing he didn't have to let Sandy ride his new fire truck.

At lunchtime Evan said his teacher told him books were his friends. He also said he would not come home right after school.

"Where are you going?" Mother asked.

"To the playground. We've got a Secret Society meeting."

"Be sure you're home by five," Mother said.

While Sandy napped Abbot looked at his books. How could a book be his friend if he didn't know what the letters said? He pushed the books onto the floor.

Sandy woke up cranky. There was nothing Abbot wanted to do. If he were big like Evan he could just be home by five. He found Mother in the kitchen. "May I go to the school playground?" he asked.

"If you're home by five."

Abbot straightened his shoulders. He tossed a careless "so long" to Sandy, who was riding his fire truck again.

Abbot knew the way to the playground well. Around the corner, past the hydrant, at the end of the street where the Murphys lived. The Murphys were old and didn't have children, but they had a huge orange dog that Father said was too darn big to be a lap dog. Goldie often came to visit. Once Abbot had let the big dog lick him from toes to chin. Abbot waved to Goldie as he passed her yard.

At the playground he saw a lot of children, but he didn't see Evan.

There was a long line at the high slide. Abbot waited at the end. The children talked and laughed. No one talked to him. When Abbot finally got to the steps a big girl with dark bangs pushed in front.

"You're too little," she said, and went up the ladder.

"Yeah, kid, you're too little." A tall boy followed the girl.

"I'm bigger," Abbot said. No one heard him. Suddenly he was at the end of the line again. Where was Evan?

He hunted all over. He found Evan and three friends behind the backstop in a circle, drawing strange pictures in the sand. Abbot stood outside the circle.

Finally he said, "Can I play?"

Mike said, "It's the kid brother."

"Go on home, Abbot," Evan said. "I told you this was a secret meeting. It's private."

At home, Abbot knew, Sandy would be on the fire truck. He'd push him off and Sandy would cry. Then Mother would say, Why did you make Sandy cry? Yet he didn't want to be here either.

Abbot found a shady doorway and watched the children in the sun. His throat started to ache. He pressed his lips tight together, closed his eyes, hunched his shoulders, and waited to see what would happen.

What happened was a lot of yelling and barking.

"Look out!" someone cried.

"Here he comes!"

"There he goes!"

Abbot opened his eyes. Some children ran out of the playground. Some huddled against the wall. Others ran in circles waving their arms. Goldie leaped and bounded happily among them. The more the children yelled, the more she barked and chased them.

When the big dog ran close, Abbot said, "Goldie!" very firmly.

The dog stopped, turned, and trotted to Abbot. He let her lick his whole arm. Then he took her collar. Leaning against her, Abbot led his soft orange friend out of the playground.

As he closed the gate he heard the big girl say, "Gee, thanks, kid. You're brave!"

"Don't thank me," Abbot said. "Thank Mr. Nobody."

Mother couldn't get used to Mr. Nobody, but Abbot got used to Evan being off at school the way you get used to brushing your teeth. There was hardly any trouble till Halloween.

For weeks Abbot and Evan had planned their costumes and where they'd go after dark. But Halloween was here and Abbot sat under the kitchen table trying to think. How could he ever make Mother understand how big he was?

"Only babies cry," Evan told him. Abbot knew he wasn't a baby, but when Mother said he couldn't go out after dark he got what Father called his thundercloud face on. Abbot couldn't help the face.

"I'm *not* a baby," Abbot said, but it sounded wrong.

Mother tried to coax him out from under the table. "Here's your bag. You may ring doorbells on this side of the street now while it's light."

"No thanks," said Abbot. "Witches don't come out till dark."

"But cats do, and your costume is all ready."

10

"The cat face makes my nose itch."

Evan came in. Mother said, "You look wonderful." Abbot saw the black paper mustache was crooked, and Evan's pirate king hat had a drip of paint on the side. The only good thing was the long silver wooden sword Father had made.

"You wouldn't scare a flea," Abbot said.

"What's the matter with Abbot?"

"He's mad because he has to wait until he's older before he can go out at night."

Abbot knew there was no point in waiting. He'd measured himself on the yardstick Father had nailed to the cellar wall. He was no bigger than he'd been on his birthday.

Evan kneeled close to Abbot. "Don't be mad. I'll give you some of my candy. Just give me your bag and . . ."

Abbot had an idea. He beckoned Evan under the table and whispered.

"What mischief are you boys up to?"

"What's mischief?" Sandy asked.

"Something I hope you never learn," Mother said. As they crawled out Abbot's eyes felt shiny. He wasn't going to mind staying home now.

"You know, you might need a stick," he said to Evan.

"I can use my sword."

Evan might be bigger, Abbot decided, but he knew a good idea when he heard one.

Abbot and Sandy were already in bed when they heard

11

Father's big shoes clump, clump up the stairs.

As Father bent to kiss him good night, Abbot asked, "How long will it be till I'm older?"

"If you think about it too much it will take forever."

When Abbot was sure Sandy was asleep he got the long rope from the closet and tied it to last year's Easter basket. He let the basket out the window. Then he waited, watching and listening.

It wasn't like the usual night outside his window. Though it was dark, there were lights in the doorways. Things moved on the black street below, funny figures with hats and tails. He could see strange faces when they crossed under the streetlamp. For an awful moment Abbot wished he were out, but then he closed his eyes and hugged his knees. He pretended to be Mr. Nobody, who was with Evan.

A real ghost roamed the winding streets that night, ringing doorbells, whispering from the bushes. At each house the bell rang; when the door was opened no one was there, only a paper bag hanging in midair. A mysterious voice said, "I am Nobody. Put some candy in the bag."

Though people tried to guess who was behind the voice, no one could. Abbot Dodge, in his dark bedroom, was the only one who knew the voice from nowhere.

He waited for the signal—a whistle. He felt the rope tug between his fingers. He pulled the basket up and

fingered the goods—an orange, candy corn, bubble gum,
Tootsie Rolls, and best of all, a box of raisins.

He let the empty basket down and happily settled to
wait some more. Mr. Nobody knew he loved raisins!

4 November • How to Eat Nothing

One Wednesday morning Abbot and Sandy watched three men carry beds and chairs and tables out of the Burgesses' house next door and pack everything into a van. Abbot peeked in at the strangely empty rooms.

Thursday at breakfast Mother said, "Abbot, Mr. Nobody has to go, and that's final."

"Why?" asked Abbot.

"Why?" asked Evan.

"And that's final," said Sandy.

"Abbot is taking him too seriously. Yesterday three people asked me about it. He's been telling everyone he's Mr. Nobody. I don't want any nonsense about this on Thanksgiving day when my brothers are here."

"Oh, boy, Thanksgiving," said Evan. "Pumpkin pie."

"And stuffing," said Abbot.

"What do you plan to do about Mr. Nobody?" asked Father.

"You couldn't send him to bed without any supper," said Evan.

"I'll think of something," Mother said. "Abbot must

learn the difference between what is real and what is pretend."

Abbot decided although mothers were bigger and more patient than brothers, they understood less and learned more slowly. So he explained again, "He's real except you can't see him."

"All right," Mother said, "if he's real where does he live?"

Abbot grinned. "Who lives next door?"

"Nobody," Mother said.

Father raised his eyebrows; Evan and Abbot laughed.

Mother said, "I give up. Time for school."

On Thanksgiving day two aunts, two uncles, and three cousins came for dinner. There were nuts to eat and as much cider to drink as they wanted. Abbot had three helpings of stuffing. After dinner Father and the uncles talked while Abbot and Evan played cowboy with the cousins. After everyone left Mother said the children would have to go right to bed because she was exhausted.

During the night Abbot was sick. He threw up so often he didn't have time to sleep. The last time Mother tucked him back in bed he put his arms around her neck and kissed her. He decided fathers understood better but mothers were nicer when you were sick.

In the morning Abbot's stomach still hurt. He was glad Mother told him to stay in bed and not to eat anything except ginger ale and a few saltines. Abbot slept all morning. In the afternoon Father played checkers with him, and he slept some more.

He was just feeling like getting up when Mother put Sandy to bed, straightened Abbot's sheets, and said good night.

Abbot was wide awake. His bed was hot. His stomach hurt in a new way. He was hungry! He could hear voices downstairs. He smelled something good. He found Mother and Father and Evan at the dining table with no place for him.

"Hi," Evan said. "We're having more turkey."

"What are you doing out of bed?" Mother asked.

"I'm hungry."

"You may have some ginger ale and a cracker."

"I want some turkey."

"I'm sorry, dear." Her voice didn't sound sorry enough to let him eat.

"Father, may I have just one bite of your stuffing?"

Father looked at Mother, but Mother shook her head.

"I didn't have any supper." His voice was shaky.

Mother took him upstairs. "Now snuggle into bed, and you'll be all well in the morning."

"I'm all well now," said Abbot. But she went out.

Eyes wide open, Abbot thought about how hungry he was. Good food smells tickled his nose. He knew Mother wasn't being mean, but she didn't believe he was well. If he were older she'd believe him. If Father or Evan wanted something to eat they just got it. If Sandy cried she fed him. Abbot was too old to cry and too young to go and get what he wanted.

His throat began to ache in the old warning way, so he shut his eyes and . . .

"What would you do if you couldn't have anything to eat?" he asked out loud.

"I'd eat nothing."

Abbot grinned. "I'd like a coffee ice-cream cone."

Abbot reached into the darkness, then changed his mind. He got up, cleared Sandy's cars off the table, pulled up two chairs. Sandy rolled over. Abbot sat down.

"Now the ice-cream cone, please." He took the cone from his invisible friend. He could almost feel the smooth coolness on his tongue.

"Now I'd like some stuffing," he said. "Would you?"

Abbot was so busy eating and chatting he didn't hear Mother and Father come upstairs.

Suddenly the door opened. "What are you doing up at this time of night?" they asked.

"I'm eating nothing with Mr. Nobody. He didn't get any dinner either."

17

5 December • All Mixed Up

One day Mother took Abbot and Evan on the commuter train to the city. Abbot watched out of the dusty window as houses rushed by; trees rushed by; rocks and bridges and fences rushed by.

"Everything is in a hurry except the river," he said. "The river isn't going any place at all."

"Silly," Evan said. "The river's the only thing that *is* running. Everything else is standing still. You're all mixed up."

In the city they were supposed to look at the beautiful store windows and see Santa Claus. There were so many people that all Abbot could see were ladies' coats and pocketbooks. They stood in a long line to see a messy man with a stringy beard who, Abbot knew, couldn't be Santa Claus.

The man put a bony arm around Abbot and asked him how old he was. Abbot's voice wouldn't work. He squirmed out from under the arm.

Evan said, "He's mixed up going on not mixed up. I'm nine going on ten."

All that month the more Abbot heard about Christmas the more mixed up he got. Mother said Christmas was for children, but she made lists of grown-ups they'd send cards and presents to.

The posters in store windows showed sleighs and snow, but it was so warm he didn't need to zip his coat.

Father said it was a time of peace on earth, goodwill toward men, but Mary Jane Clancy's big brother gave Evan a bloody nose and told him to get out of his yard.

Every morning Abbot asked Father if it was Christmas yet. Every morning Father said, "No, not yet. You'll have to wait a few days more." Abbot decided the bigger he got the more he had to wait for things.

Evan said, "Look at the calendar, stupid. You can see how many days there are to wait." Abbot looked at his calendar but all he saw were squares.

One afternoon Abbot was more impatient than ever, and Mother was busier than ever. "I have a million things to do," she said. "Abbot and Sandy, get out from between my feet!"

Sitting on the kitchen stool listening to Sandy singing in the next room, Abbot thought perhaps Mother was getting younger, and all mixed up.

Then she decided that as a special treat, Evan and Abbot could walk to the village to pick out their tree. Abbot was excited. He ran to measure himself. *I must be bigger,* he thought, *or she wouldn't let me go.*

The sun was out. They met some dogs and saw some

cars. At the grocery store across from the railroad station in the village they picked out the biggest tree they could find.

"It's too late to deliver it," the man said. "How will you get it home?"

"My father will drive down later," Evan said.

Abbot was proud of Evan. He acted just like a grown-up. Abbot felt grown up too.

"Let's start home," Evan said.

Abbot didn't want to go. Once home he'd feel small again. Without thinking he said, "We'll carry the tree home."

"What?" Evan started to argue. But when Abbot explained how surprised Mother and Father would be, Evan agreed.

It wasn't hard to carry at first, but as they walked the tree got heavier and heavier. Finally they had to drag it. They tugged and struggled. Abbot's chest ached. His arms were sore. His feet felt so heavy he could hardly lift them.

"Hurry," Evan said. "It's late."

"Wait a minute. I want to zip my coat." An icy wind had slipped down Abbot's neck and up his sleeves. It was suddenly dark. He fumbled with the zipper.

"Are you sure this is the way? It didn't seem so far before."

"I'm sure," Evan said. "Hurry!"

Abbot wished he were home in the warm kitchen.

21

While he worked over the zipper something strange happened. At first he didn't know what it was.

He felt it on the tip of his nose. Quietly.

Then it was something he smelled. Quietly.

There was a whisper in the trees. Quiet whisper.

When Abbot looked up he knew. And he smiled.

He held out his hand and caught a perfect snowflake.

"Look," he said to Evan. "Look." The street had a coat of white. White flecks caught in Evan's hair.

The air was soft, the cold gentle.

The birds were quiet.

And there—in sight—was the FRONT PORCH! Colored lights ran along the railing and spiraled up the columns showing the way.

"Christmas *is* here, isn't it?" Abbot said. "It did come after all."

"Silly," Evan said. "Of course it's here. Didn't you know this was Christmas Eve?"

"I was all mixed up," Abbot said.

6 January • Fort Nothing

During January the world stayed white. The houses on Abbot's street looked like drawings in his books. By the end of Evan's vacation Abbot's Christmas sled wasn't new any more. When Father came home each night he found the radiators covered with snow pants and mittens drying.

One morning Evan said, "It isn't fair. Abbot can play in the snow all day and I have to go to school." Before lunch Mother had a long talk with Evan. Abbot had never seen him so angry. He stuck out his lower lip. His eyes were shiny and his face looked sunburned. He left half his lunch on the table, stamped upstairs, and slammed his door.

"What did Evan do?" Abbot asked.

"Never mind, dear," Mother said sadly.

When Abbot finished eating he knocked on Evan's door.

No answer.

He opened the door a crack. Evan lay on his bed staring at the ceiling.

24

"What's the matter?"

"I hate parents," Evan said. "Parents are a nuisance."

Abbot thought about that. He wasn't sure he agreed. Much as he loved and admired Evan, Abbot thought Evan was a nuisance sometimes, especially when Evan wouldn't let him play. Mother said Sandy was a nuisance when he got into things like the flour. So if you thought parents and brothers were a nuisance, who in the world was left who was not a nuisance except yourself?

Finally Abbot asked, "Why?"

"I can't go out after school. Just because there are a few things I forgot to put away. Mother says I can't go out until I clean my room."

Abbot looked around. Clothes, games, pencils, papers, wood shavings, were all over the floor. "Why don't you clean it up?" he asked.

"It'll take too long. By the time I finish Mike and David will have the snow fort all done. It isn't fair. Mother doesn't make you clean your room."

"Sometimes in the morning I help," said Abbot. He felt sorry for Evan. Maybe being bigger wasn't always best. Still, Evan had stayed up till midnight on New Year's Eve. Abbot was mixed up again.

Mother called from downstairs. "Evan, time to go back to school."

"You see?" said Evan. "I never can do anything I want." Abbot heard him stamping as he put on his big black boots. Then Abbot went to his own room.

He didn't look at his books. He thought about Evan's anger, and about the snow fort they would build. *When I am angry,* Abbot thought, *I shut my eyes and pretend to be Mr. Nobody.*

Abbot closed his eyes . . .

Quietly, so as not to wake Sandy or disturb Mother, who was having coffee, Mr. Nobody tiptoed into Evan's room. He worked fast and sometimes things fell.

"Who's making noise?" Mother called once.

"Nobody," Abbot answered.

After a while Mother came upstairs. Abbot said, "May Evan play in the snow when he gets home? It wouldn't be fun without him."

"He has to clean his room," Mother said.

"Why?" Abbot asked.

"It's a terrible mess," said Mother.

"It is?" asked Abbot. "I didn't see anything wrong."

Mother marched him down the hall. "Look again," she said. Then, "Oh!" Then, "Who—"

Abbot grinned. Suddenly she hugged him so tight he couldn't breathe.

"It's wonderful of you to help Evan." Her voice sounded fuzzy. "You, Abbot. Not some person you made up who isn't real."

"It's not some person," Abbot said. "It's no person. Nobody."

That afternoon Abbot and Evan and Mike and David built the biggest snow fort for miles around, with sides so

26

high Abbot couldn't see over the top. Evan made a sign.
It said,

FORT NOTHING
PLEASE NOBODY ENTER

It seemed the winter's gray cold would never end. Abbot was tired of putting on boots and mittens and scarf and hat. He was tired of hiding from the bitter wind in the snow fort until his nose and toes were numb. He was tired of taking off boots and mittens and scarf and hat.

A new girl named Carolyn Magill moved into the house next door. Mother was glad, she said, because Abbot wouldn't be staring into the empty rooms. Though Abbot liked Carolyn all right, he worried about where Mr. Nobody lived now.

One sunny afternoon Mother took them ice-skating. It was pretty at the pond. Sun shone through the two pine trees on the little island and glittered in stripes across the ice.

Mother laced up Evan's old hockey skates on Abbot. When he stood up his legs trembled. The ice seemed miles away. Double runners had never felt like this! Carefully he slid one foot forward. He tried to glide. The ice rushed up and whanged his head and the trees spun. He watched skates and legs flash by until he felt the cold

28

through his pants. Evan helped him up, saying, "Fall on your knees next time. It doesn't hurt so much."

He tried to glide again and finally reached the island after only six knee falls. He rested, poking the edge of the ice with the toe of his skate. He watched Sandy shuffle along on his old double runners. Abbot's head hurt. His ankles ached and his toes were frozen. He got to his feet once more and scrambled his way back to the shore.

"Come and get me!" Evan shouted. Abbot climbed off the ice. David and the other boys whizzed by after Evan, laughing and falling on purpose. Their laughter seemed very far away, like Mother's and Father's on company nights, echoing up the stairs.

"What's the matter?" Mother asked him.

"Nothing." Then Abbot said, "How old were you when you learned to skate?"

"About your age, I guess. Maybe a little older."

She rubbed his cold hands. He unlaced his skates. "Don't worry," she said. "Next year it will be easier."

Abbot knew perfectly well next year would never come. Just like tomorrow. Evan had told him, "Tomorrow never comes." What Abbot cared about was this year, right now.

And right now he didn't feel like skating. He felt like getting warm and going exploring.

When he was in his shoes again the hard ground felt so good! He ran along the riverbank until he was breathless. He crossed a little wooden bridge and climbed the rock on the other side. Hidden behind the boulder was a wooden shack with no glass in the window and an old wooden door. He pushed the door open. Inside there was a bench, a round black stove, a broken flowerpot, and some sticks. It was nice inside, and the cold wind couldn't touch him. He was as happy as the day he caught his first moth. He had found Mr. Nobody's house.

He stuffed some sticks in the stove, pulled the bench over, and pretended to light the fire. He heard Mother calling, but he did not answer. It was so nice here where nobody lived and nobody talked, where no one asked questions, where there was no waiting. He could feel the fire on his face, and the good hot tea warmed him down to his toes.

Mother called again. He would have to go back. He wanted to tell them about the house, but he needed a way to tell so that Evan wouldn't make it *his* house. He hummed a tune as he walked back along the river.

They were all glad to see him.

"Where were you?" Mother said. "I called and called. Aren't you cold?"

"No," said Abbot. "I got warmed all right."

"How?" Evan asked. His teeth were chattering.

Abbot sang the song he'd made up.

> There is a house where Nobody is,
> And Nobody knows where Nobody lives.
> No one or nothing that someone can see

But me and Mr. Nobody.
Nobody's house is high on a rock.
When someone is there, he is not.
When Nobody's there we have tea,
Me and Mr. Nobody.

"Where's the house?" asked Evan. "When can I see it?"
"Where somebody isn't," Abbot said. "It could be anywhere. Maybe Nobody will take you tomorrow."

8 March • Making Something out of Nothing

"Is it spring yet?" Abbot asked Father.

"Not yet," Father said.

"Spring is just around the corner," said Mother.

At the front corner of the house Abbot found a pile of snow. At the garage corner long icicles hung from the gutter. It didn't look or smell or feel like spring.

Yet Father bought fertilizer for the lawn, and Mother washed curtains. Evan talked about his birthday, which was on the first day of spring.

Abbot and Carolyn Magill found a dead robin in the snow. Carolyn said it must have starved, so they put out breadcrumbs for other birds that had flown north too early, and they buried the robin. Abbot patted the new grave with his mitten. Suddenly he saw something yellow coming through a patch of snow.

"Look!" He showed the crocus to Carolyn.

"Spring is just around the corner," Carolyn said.

On the first day of spring Evan woke Abbot saying, "You have to be nice to me today."

"Happy birthday," Abbot said.

"I'm nice," said Sandy.

There were two presents. Evan opened the big one first. It was a game of Parcheesi. "Oh, boy," said Abbot. "Can I play?"

"Later. It's my present so I have to use it first."

Inside the little box was a knife, a real jackknife. Abbot watched Evan smile. They had talked many times about owning knives. Evan ran to get a piece of wood. Father gave Evan a lesson on how to use his knife. Abbot listened.

When Father finished Abbot said, "Will I get a knife for my birthday?"

"You're still too young," Father said. "Knives are dangerous."

"Oh," said Abbot and swallowed hard.

All day Evan showed off his knife—to Carolyn, to Sandy, Mother, David, and Michael, and all the friends who came to his party. Abbot swallowed many times. He watched Evan unwrap the mountain of presents. Evan wouldn't let him touch anything. By afternoon he didn't like Evan very much. That made him sad. You were supposed to like someone on his birthday, especially your brother.

Abbot did like the icing on Evan's cake, and the model airplane he found at his place. But whenever he thought about Evan's knife his throat ached. Finally he went to the bathroom for a drink of water. He stared at his own face in the mirror. It didn't look very different from

Evan's face. It looked plenty old enough to have a knife.

"It isn't fair," he said. "Evan gets older and older and I just stay the same."

What did you do if you wanted something so much you couldn't think about anything else, even nice things?

Abbot closed his eyes and . . .

Outside he hunted for just the right kind of stick. He sat on the porch and thought about what he could whittle if he had a knife.

That didn't work. He threw the stick away.

He asked Mr. Nobody for a knife. Remembering Father's lesson, Abbot opened the knife. Ever so careful to push the blade away from himself, he began to carve his pretend wood with his invisible knife.

Soon Carolyn came along. "What are you doing?" she asked.

"Whittling."

"Oh," said Carolyn.

"Do you want a knife?"

"Okay," said Carolyn. She sat beside him.

"Me too," Sandy said.

"Be careful," Abbot told him. "Knives are very dangerous."

David found them on the porch. "What're you doing?" he asked.

"Whittling."

"You don't even have anything in your hands." David sounded disgusted, but he didn't go away.

Finally Abbot said, "Does your mother let you have a knife?"

"No."

"Well, you might not be able to make as good a dinosaur as mine, but you could try."

"Maybe I could make a dog," David said.

By five o'clock Evan and Mike were there too. Evan had bandages on three fingers. His real knife was in his pocket. He was carving an elephant, he said.

Father came up the walk and asked what they were doing. They all talked at once. Abbot saw Father was mixed up.

"You mean," said Father, "you're all making something out of nothing?"

"Yes," said Abbot. "And I didn't cut myself once."

Father thought a minute, then said, "Lend me your knife, please, Evan."

Father shaved a piece of wood until it was all gone but the pile of shavings. "Well," he said, "aren't you going to ask what I'm doing?"

"What are you doing?" they asked.

"I'm making nothing out of something," Father said.

9 April • Is Nothing Too Small to See?

In April it rained and rained and rained. Water ran down the windows and overflowed the gutters. Abbot's neck got wet whenever he stepped out the back door.

Evan came home one afternoon with his yellow rain slicker all brown. His hat was brown, even his face was brown. He hollered at Abbot to come outside. Evan showed him a mud puddle as deep as the third buckle on Abbot's boots.

Evan took a running start and slid clear from one end of the puddle to the other. Abbot discovered he could slide even farther than Evan.

"That's because you don't weigh so much." Evan knew the reason for everything.

Next morning Evan was sick with a sore throat and an earache. It was still raining. Evan stayed in bed a whole week. When he wasn't sleeping he was hurting. When Mother wasn't cooking or taking Evan medicine or talking to the doctor she was looking worried.

With the rain and no one to play with except Sandy, Abbot thought he might as well be sick too. He went to bed but he didn't feel sick, so he found Mother in the kitchen.

"May I play with Evan?"

"For the ninety-ninth time, Abbot, NO. Stay out of Evan's room. I don't want you catching his germs."

"I looked but I couldn't see any germs."

"They're all over, but they're invisible."

"Like Mr. Nobody?"

"No. The germs are real and can make you sick. Now let me finish this custard. Later if I have time we'll color some eggs."

"How are we going to hunt eggs if it doesn't stop raining?" Abbot asked.

When Evan woke up he said, "How am I going to hunt eggs if I can't get out of bed?"

Mother said if it was still raining they'd hunt eggs in the house. If Evan's ear stopped aching he could get up long enough to hunt them.

The day before Easter Abbot was sad; Evan was cranky; Sandy was noisy; Mother was tired. She told Sandy and Abbot to go to their room so she could have some peace and quiet. Abbot watched the rain.

"It doesn't matter so much to you," he said to Sandy. "You're too young to know what you're missing."

"What am I missing?"

Abbot kicked a slipper under his bed. There were some things, like the smell of baby grass, digging up the first earthworm, or finding a purple egg in the folds of the

38

early tulip leaves, that he couldn't explain. But Evan knew. That's why he was so cranky and ordered everyone around.

If only he could talk to Evan! But he wasn't allowed in Evan's room because of the germs, the tiny invisible germs. He closed his eyes and . . .

"Oh-oh, there you go again," Sandy said.

But Abbot wasn't going anywhere. He was listening to the rain and trying to understand about the germs. So small they were invisible—like nothing! Was nothing too small to see? How did the germs make Evan's ear ache? Abbot saw some dust on the table and blew it, watching the particles fly up and around, then slowly settle again. Were germs like dust, only smaller? How could you get rid of things too small to see?

He watched the rain driving past the window, leaves flying past too, now, as the wind came up whining and whistling. The wind music made Abbot begin to think of another song. He sang it in his head a couple of times, and finally out loud for Sandy.

> Blow, wind, blow!
> Blow Evan's germs away.
> Shine, sun, shine
> For Easter day!

Then while Sandy went on singing, Abbot closed his eyes and thought of Mr. Nobody, who could go anywhere

39

and do anything. He could go even into Evan's room without catching the germs!

Early, early on Easter morning a ray of sun touched Evan's eyelid. He listened to the wind. He thought he heard someone singing. He saw a tall chocolate rabbit with a bow tie beside his bed. The rabbit must be singing, he thought fuzzily, and went back to sleep.

When he woke later he saw the rabbit was really there. The hickory leaves were shining in the sun. He turned his head. His ear didn't hurt!

Evan called to Abbot, who happened to be right at the door. "I'm well," Evan said. "Let's go hunt eggs."

"I know," Abbot said. "I thought you'd never wake up. The wind must have blown all your germs away."

At that Sandy, who was standing behind Abbot, sang, "Blow, wind, blow!" in his loudest voice.

Mother and Father came to find out what the racket was all about, and how Evan felt this morning.

"Who made up that song?" Mother asked.

"Dr. Nobody," they all answered at once.

"Last one up the beech tree's a rotten you-know-what." Evan yelled, raced across the yard, and swung himself up to the first branch. All of them, Mike and David and Jeffrey, ran too. Abbot was last, but he was used to that. He held tight to the swinging rope and pushed his feet against the trunk. He hooked one foot over the lowest branch. How did you get the other one up? He slipped.

Finally Evan said, "I'll give you a boost." He climbed down and pushed on Abbot's rear so that Abbot could get both feet over the branch. Abbot sat hugging the trunk, breathless and proud.

"Go on up," Evan said.

Abbot looked up to the next branch. Then he looked down. The ground was far away.

"What's the matter?"

"I've changed my mind. I don't want to."

"You're just a baby," David said from someplace higher.

Abbot couldn't think of anything to say.

"Well, come on down then," said Evan.

"I can't."

"Hold on with your hands and let your feet go."

"It's too far."

"Well, go on up, then."

"No," said Abbot.

Evan was getting impatient. Abbot didn't know what to do. If he were invisible he'd be able to get away from all of them. He closed his eyes. He clenched his teeth and let go. The bark scraped his hands and his knee banged on a rock.

He watched Evan climb into the tree again. It looked so easy! "Never mind," Mike said. "You'll do it okay when you're bigger."

"I *am* bigger," Abbot said so quietly no one heard. His knee and his hands hurt, and he was hungry. He closed his eyes and . . .

"Have a cookie," Mr. Nobody said.

"Thanks." Abbot took one from the box that wasn't there, and let it soften in his mouth.

Feeling better, he walked past the red velvet tulips. He watched a bee buzz right into the fuzzy black stamens in the center.

He lay on the thick new grass and looked at the sky. The boys yelled at each other high in the tree. It was taller than the house. He wished he hadn't been so scared. He squeezed his eyes shut. Mr. Nobody could go to the top. He could go to the sky!

43

Abbot rolled onto his stomach. When he opened his eyes he was staring into two little black eyes on the sides of a little brown head that looked like a cigar. Abbot laughed.

"Hello, where did you come from?" The turtle didn't answer. "From nowhere?"

The turtle poked its head out of its shell a little farther. Abbot gently touched the nose, and the head jerked back. Abbot waited. Slowly the head came out again.

"Would you like a cookie?" Abbot asked.

The turtle didn't answer, but it didn't move either.

"Would you like to live in my house?" Abbot asked.

By the time Evan and his friends came down from the tree, Abbot's turtle was in a carton Mother had found and was eating lettuce and hamburger.

"What do you have?" Evan asked.

"A box turtle," Abbot said proudly.

"May I hold him?"

"May I see him?"

"May I look at him?"

"He's mine," Abbot said, and showed them the hinge on the turtle's lower shell that it could close and be all inside its own shell house.

"Gosh, Abbot, you're lucky." Abbot looked at Evan a minute, then handed him the turtle. "You may hold him if you want."

Evan examined the turtle carefully. "He's nice," he

said. "If you feed him maybe he'll stay in our yard." Evan seemed to think a minute. "I guess you wouldn't have found him if you'd gotten up in the tree. Turtles can't climb trees either."

Abbot smiled and put his new pet back in the carton. Brothers were sometimes almost as nice as turtles, he thought.

11 June • Which Way Is Down?

Things happened fast. Sandy had a birthday and got his own dump truck. Abbot learned to count to fifty. Evan got on the fourth-grade baseball team. The poppies opened their big orange petals. One Friday night Father and Mother packed a lot of things in the car, and they all drove so long Abbot fell asleep.

He woke up when Mother said, "We're in Vermont." All Abbot could see were stars.

In the morning Abbot and Sandy and Evan went exploring. They found a wood stove in the kitchen, a wood-shed filled with logs, an axe, some old inner tubes. Outside, the grass was long and wet, the fields wide. The maple tree in the yard was so big that even holding hands they couldn't reach around the trunk. They counted nine brown-and-white cows.

There were two red barns and an old chicken house that formed three sides of a corral. In one barn they found an old sleigh, some ropes, and lots of hay. They jumped in the hay until they were sneezing and itchy.

"I hope we never go home," Abbot said. "I love Vermont."

But Sunday night they loaded the car. The cows watched them drive away. "The cows don't want us to go," Abbot said.

"We'll come back next weekend," Mother said. "And after school is out we'll stay all summer. Father will come weekends. We'll fix the chicken house so you and Evan can sleep there."

"Oh, boy," said Evan. "You'd better give us a good flashlight."

"May I bring my turtle?" asked Abbot.

"If you leave Mr. Nobody home," Mother said. Abbot hadn't thought about him all weekend.

By the time Evan's school was out there were six calves on wobbly legs that played together like children. The cows were so tame Abbot and Evan could feed them and pat their white faces.

Abbot was sad on Sunday night as he watched Father's plane become a speck in the sky.

Monday morning Evan said, "I wish Father were here so we could go for a walk."

"I'm here," said Abbot.

"You can't walk fast enough."

Abbot didn't answer.

Mother said, "Evan, while Father's away you'll have to get used to doing things with Abbot. Don't run ahead of him. Keep the house in sight. I'll ring the cowbell later and we'll drive to the river for a swim."

"Oh, all right," Evan said. They started up the hill behind the house. Abbot ran to keep up with Evan. At the woods they looked back.

"The house got smaller," Abbot said.

"That's because it is so far away," Evan said. He didn't sound grumpy any more.

They didn't mean to go so deep into the woods, but there was a wild-animal hole in the ground to investigate, and a dead birch with some good white bark. Father said it was all right to peel bark off a dead tree. They saw a deer, but when they tried to follow it the deer disappeared.

When they turned around the house was gone too.

"I can't see our house," Abbot said.

"It's down the hill. I know. I walked here with Father."

Evan turned over a log. A million tiny bugs scurried away. *You never know what you'll find in the woods,* Abbot thought.

He heard a faint tinkling sound. "There's the cowbell." Evan started down the hill.

"Wait for me," Abbot said.

"Hurry." At the bottom of the hill they started up again. "Funny," Evan said. "I don't remember going up a hill to get home."

"Are we lost?"

"Not yet." They climbed the next hill. Thick wild roses

48

and huckleberry bushes scratched Abbot's face, and he couldn't see. He rubbed his cheek and stopped to rest.

"Abbot!" Evan shouted. Abbot pushed through the bushes. "Oh, there you are. I couldn't see you."

Abbot said in his bravest voice, "You'll find the way. You walked here with Father."

"Not here."

"Oh," said Abbot.

They clawed their way through the bushes and started downhill again. So long as they kept going down, Evan said, they would be all right. Suddenly they were at the edge of the woods. The bright sunlight startled them.

"Now we should see the house," Evan said. But all they could see were rows and rows of cornstalks.

"Which way should we go?" asked Abbot.

"Down," said Evan.

"Which way is that? With so much corn I don't even know which way is down!"

"It's hard to tell." Abbot saw Evan's eyes were big. If Evan was scared then he should be too.

"I wish I really was Mr. Nobody," Abbot said. "He'd find the way home."

"Why don't you sort of ask him?" Evan said in a shaky voice.

Abbot closed his eyes and thought about his friend who could go everywhere and see everything and never get lost. He heard a car. Yesterday on the way to the airport Father had said, "How high the corn has grown!"

"Evan?"

"What?"

"If this is the same cornfield we drove by with Father, it goes to the road. If we got to the road we'd know the way home. I just heard a car!"

"That's right," said Evan. "So did I."

Running between the rows of corn, Abbot didn't worry about Evan getting ahead. On the long climb up the driveway Evan waited for Abbot to catch up. He said, "I'm sure glad you came with me. I would have been lost without you."

One steaming day Mr. Groley, the farmer who owned the cows, brought a young bull over in a truck. He warned Evan, "Now you'd best stay out of the pasture with the bull in there. He's not mean, only a year old, but he might not be friendly like the cows."

After Mr. Groley left, Evan said he wasn't scared of any old bull. The baby bull ate salt right out of Evan's hand!

At dinner Abbot was so tired and felt so floppy he couldn't eat. He slipped under the table. Laughing, Sandy kicked him. Mother said supper was over. Right then. Before she put the cookies on.

They walked across the night-black space to the chicken house and crawled into bed. In his narrow canvas army cot Abbot was wide awake.

"Sometimes mothers are mean."

"I know," said Evan. "But they're nice sometimes too."

"When?"

"Today. Father was too busy reading so Mother took us swimming."

"That's true." Abbot could smell the barn. A cow

51

mooed close by. He could see stars outside the square hole in the wall that was the window. "But I wish I had a cookie."

"I wish I knew why the cows were making so much noise."

Suddenly there was a loud moo outside their window. "Abbot, there's a cow in the yard! Did you leave the gate open?"

"No," said Abbot.

Evan was already at the window. "It's the bull, and he's right here!" Abbot ran to the opening. The white-faced bull stood calmly eating the front lawn.

"What'll we do?" Abbot whispered.

"Get a rope and put him back in the corral."

"How?"

The cows were making a terrific racket. "If we don't," Evan said, "all the cows will follow him."

"Mr. Groley says they only follow the lead cow."

"But Mr. Groley says lots of things that don't happen," Evan reminded him. "Like telling us it never rains in Vermont. It rained three days last week."

The bull looked up at them, put his front hoofs out, and danced. "Father!" Evan and Abbot yelled.

The bull bellowed. The chicken house shook.

Evan fumbled in the dark for the rope he'd taken from the barn.

The light went on at the house. Mother and Father opened the front door, saw the bull.

"Stay where you are," Father called. "I'll chase him back."

"Careful!" Mother cried.

Father walked in a wide circle around the bull. The bull watched him. Father clapped his hands. "Go on, boy, move!"

Abbot's heart pounded. The bull put his front feet out, lowered his head, and galloped straight for Father. Mother screamed. Father stepped out of the way just in time. The bull crashed into the fence at the far end of the yard, rattling the old boards.

"Let him go," Mother called.

"I've got a rope," Evan yelled. "Shall I bring it?"

"No. Stay where you are. . . . *Just don't move.*" Father's words sounded like stones. Father walked toward the corral.

Abbot's eyes burned. He squeezed them shut and wished he were Mr. Nobody who would go to the barn and . . .

Angrily Abbot opened his eyes. Mr. Nobody couldn't help him now. That bull was real! Pretending would never get what he wanted from the barn. Yet it was a good idea. He held his breath and wished for bravery. While Evan was busy watching Father, and Father was busy watching the bull, Abbot tiptoed down the steps to the yard. The bull moved away from the fence.

Abbot ran through the open gate, past the cows in the corral, and into the barn. He stopped to catch his breath.

Where had they left the pail that morning? He couldn't see. Hay prickled his bare feet. He felt his way along the rough walls until he came to the stall where the pail might be. He put his hand down. It went right into the salt.

The pail was heavy. He struggled with it as he felt his way out. Cows nuzzled him as he crossed the corral. Finally he got through the yard and found Evan still at the window.

"I've got the salt," he whispered. "You could give it to the bull."

"What?"

"He would come to you."

"Father said to stay here."

"But the bull doesn't like Father," Abbot pleaded. "You've got to do it."

"How'd you get it? Mr. . . ."

"No," Abbot interrupted angrily. "I got it. Me! Myself! It's on the stairs."

"Okay," Evan said. "I'll try."

Abbot held his breath until he saw Evan climb onto the gate. "Here boy, here bull," Evan called gently.

"Go back!" Father yelled.

"Here boy." Evan held the pail of salt high.

"Give me that pail!" Father took three big strides toward the corral. The bull trotted after Father. Mother cried out.

"Here boy, here bull," Evan called again.

The bull lifted his nose, sniffed, then slowly walked toward the gate. As the bull came close Evan swung the pail inside the corral and dropped it. The bull trotted through the gate. Father ran and shut it, lifted Evan down, and hugged him.

Mother came out, crying, "I was so scared!"

"So was I," said Evan.

Abbot sat in the window, his feet dangling.

Finally Father said, "How did you get the salt?"

"I didn't," Evan said. "Abbot did."

"Oh, no," Mother said. "Don't tell me Abbot sent Mr. Nobody!"

"No," said Evan. "Abbot thought of the salt. Abbot got it. He told me how to call the bull. So he's the brave one."

"Abbot?" Mother and Father looked at him.

Abbot's throat ached in a new, strangely nice way, like when you tell someone you love him a lot.

"Come on down," Mother said softly.

They went inside and Mother made tea. Everyone talked about how brave Abbot and Evan were. It seemed to Abbot that his chest was too big for him, and that Mother knew it. He felt much older and wiser than he had that morning.

Suddenly Father asked, "Who did leave the gate open, anyway?"

Someone, somewhere, whispered, "Mr. Nobody."

There were patches of red on the maples. The wind blew through the chicken house so hard they needed extra blankets. Father said he had cut enough stove wood to last until they went home.

Going home, to Abbot, meant the end of summer, the end of everything in the world that was good.

He thought about the good summer things; swimming in the river even when it rained. Evan told him, the bigger you get the better you float, and now Abbot could swim halfway across the river, so it must be true. Abbot thought of walks in the woods, late dinners when Father cooked outside, sleeping with Evan in the chicken house, feeding the cows early in the morning when the pasture was wet with dew, long rainy afternoons by the fire, playing cards, hearing stories, popping corn.

Best of all was the Night Out. Until the very last minute Abbot was sure he wouldn't be allowed to go. Mother fixed a picnic supper. Father rolled some blankets. Evan kept saying, "I've got my knife." Abbot didn't say anything. If he had to stay home with Mother and Sandy he wouldn't want to talk to any of them ever again.

When the car was packed, Father asked Evan if he was all set. Evan said, "Yes, I've got my knife."

Then Father said, "Hurry, get into your dungarees, Abbot. We're waiting for you!"

They slept right on the ground at the very top of the mountain! Even the trees were way below them. Abbot tried to keep his eyes open so he could watch the moon rise, but his eyelids were so heavy. Once he blinked and saw a bear! It turned out to be only Father still sitting by the fire. The next time he opened his eyes there was a beautiful soft gray light at the edge of the sky. Evan was already up.

A pink tinge appeared at the treetops below. Abbot and Evan watched the sun come over the mountain. It moved so fast, that big orange ball. Abbot saw the sun move!

Abbot woke up in his home bed. He saw the sun stripe on the ceiling where it always was, and Sandy asleep with his little round mouth open. He saw his teddy bear, his fire truck, his telescope, his books. Everything was in its place.

The calendar was the only thing that had changed. The picture was the same spaniel that had always been there, but *something* was different.

The numbers! 1, 2, 3, 4, 5, 6, up to 31, he counted. Some in red, some in black.

He stared and stared at them. Suddenly he knew. They had always been there, but now he, Abbot Sanderson Dodge, could *read* the numbers!

And he hadn't even tried to learn.

Feeling quite important he brushed his teeth, put on clean shorts and his new striped shirt, and went into Mother's room.

"Look at me," he said.

Mother opened her eyes. "Why you're all dressed! Happy Birthday!"

"Is it really my birthday?"

"Yes," said Mother.

"May I go to the swamp?"

"Pretty soon."

"And cross the street?"

"If you're careful."

"And go to school with Evan?"

"School starts next week."

Abbot thought about seeing the numbers. Now he would find out what the letters in his books meant, too. "How did I get bigger without even trying?" he said.

"You just grew," Mother said.

Abbot looked over his shoulder, saw himself in the long mirror. He might even measure up to the red line at the roller coaster now.

Tomorrow did come after all, he thought.